The Fence Was Too High

Story by Olivia Esh

Illustrations by Rhonda Childress

RSVP

RAINTREE
STECK-VAUGHN
PUBLISHERS
The Steck-Vaughn Company

Austin, Texas

Story Link Program®

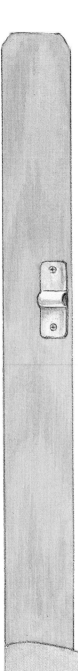
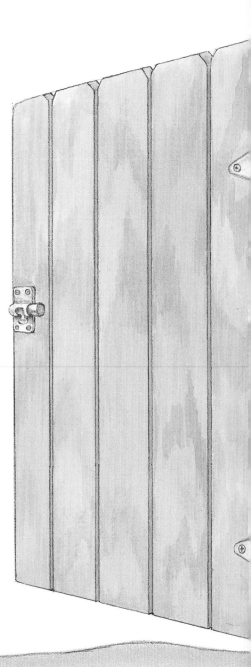

To all my friends and classmates as we grow and make our discoveries together. — O.E.

To my mom and dad for all their love and encouragement. — R.C.

Printed in Mexico.

1 2 3 4 5 6 7 8 9 0 RRD 98 97 96 95 94 93

Library of Congress Cataloging-in-Publication Data

Esh, Olivia, 1983–
  The fence was too high / written by Olivia Esh; illustrated by Rhonda Childress.
    p.   cm. (Publish-a-book)
    Summary: Oliver is frustrated that he cannot see over the fence around his back yard, until another year passes and he finds that he has grown.
    ISBN 0–8114–4460–0
    1. Children's writings, American. [1. Size — Fiction.   2. Growth — Fiction.   3. Fences — Fiction.   4. Children's writings.]
I. Childress, Rhonda, ill.   II. Title.   III. Series.
PZ7.E7458Fe   1994   93-34499
[E] — dc20   CIP
                                                AC

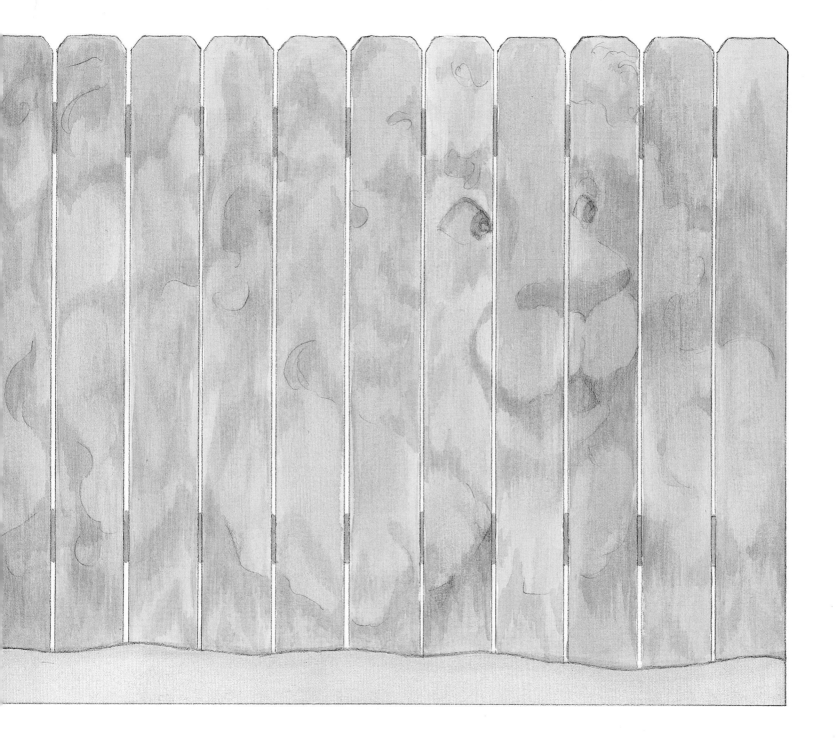

Oliver loved playing in his back yard. He loved the way the grass tickled his bare feet. He liked watching the bees fly from flower to flower and the ants making their anthills. He liked picking the buttercups and twisting them on his nose. And most of all he liked his sandbox. He would sit there playing and wiggling his toes and fingers in the warm sand.

The one thing Oliver didn't like about his yard was the wood plank fence. Oliver's sandbox was close to the fence, and he could hear noises on the other side. Sometimes that frightened him. He told his parents about the noises, but they said, "It's just the neighbors." Oliver wanted to see for himself, but the fence was too high!

As Oliver played, he could hear scratching and growling noises. "Maybe it's a bear or a lion," he imagined. He couldn't tell for sure because the fence was too high!

Oliver tried looking through the fence, but it was impossible. He tried climbing the fence. He fell. He even tried digging under the fence. But he only had a plastic play shovel, and it took too long.

Oliver asked his parents if they could make the fence lower.

"Oliver," they said, "the fence isn't really too tall. Someday you'll discover that."

Oliver spent the summer playing in his sandbox, wondering what might be on the other side of that fence.

Before he knew it, it was growing colder outside, and it was time to cover the sandbox. Oliver started school, and there wasn't much time for playing outdoors.

Finally summer arrived and it was time to uncover the sandbox once again.

As Oliver began playing in the sand, he started hearing the same old noises coming from the other side of the fence. Oliver stood up. He could see over the fence! Oliver knew immediately where the scratching and growling noises had come from. The neighbor's dog was on the opposite side of the fence. Oliver was very excited.

7 years —

6½ years —

6 years —

5½ years —

5 years —

4½ years —

4 years —

18

"Mom," he said, "the fence is lower. I can see over it now!"

"I think you have just made an important discovery," Oliver's mother said. "The fence hasn't changed. You have."

Oliver was amazed. He had been growing and changing all the time. What a discovery!

Oliver noticed many more changes that summer. He could see out the kitchen window now. And his feet touched the floor in the car. These were good changes. He also discovered that his legs had become too long for his bike. And he couldn't fit into his favorite hiding place under the bed quite as easily anymore. Oliver wasn't sure he liked those changes.

Oliver was growing up. Things are always changing. But Oliver will never forget the summer he made his greatest discovery. The fence wasn't too high!

Olivia Esh, author of **The Fence Was Too High**, has enjoyed reading books for as long as she can remember. Having a story of her own published is a dream come true. Olivia attributes her love of books to her family. Her parents, Michael and Sharon, and her older sister, Rebecca, are avid readers and encourage reading in their home in the small town of Reedsville, Pennsylvania. Olivia acknowledges her grandparents, Lee and Doris Longwell, Phyllis Esh, and the late Guy Esh, who have always provided Olivia with support and encouragement. Olivia also credits the teachers and staff at Sacred Heart School in Lewiston, Pennsylvania, for supporting creativity and providing a caring environment.

Olivia is an excellent student and a member of the gifted program at her school. She likes to keep busy. In the evenings and on weekends, Olivia attends piano lessons, studies ballet and jazz at Miss Judy's School of Dance, and represents Perry-Juniata Gym as a competitive gymnast.

In regard to her future, Olivia's dreams include teaching school and writing books during the summer. Olivia has a great love of animals and someday hopes to have many pets. She has a Lhasa apso dog named Rocke and four cats named Jazzmine, Razzmine, Pazzmine, and Tazzmine.

When asked to name her favorite place, Olivia always answers "home." She loves the small town of Reedsville and has no desire to live anywhere else. "My family is here, my friends are here, and I can walk to Pap and Nan's (her grandparents' house) whenever I want. I love it here."

The ten honorable-mention winners in the **1993 Raintree/Steck-Vaughn Young Publish-a-Book Contest** were Alisha Ayers, Elydale Elementary, Ewing, Virginia; Matthew Fuller, Leoma Elementary, Leoma, Tennessee; Matthew Clapper, Liberty Memorial Library, Grafton, Wisconsin; Robert Grau, Clifton Lawrence School, Sussex, New Jersey; Kamal Simpson, Irvington Public Library, Irvington, New Jersey; Raven Burke, McDade Classical School, Chicago, Illinois; Diane Kalin, New Hope Elementary, New Hope, Minnesota; Ashley Raynor, North Zulch Schools, North Zulch, Texas; Amanda Morrison, Hillsborough Public Library, Neshanic, New Jersey; and Nathalie Turcios, Bateman School, Chicago, Illinois.

Rhonda Childress graduated from the University of Texas with a degree in fine arts. She now lives in Smithville, a small town near Austin, with her husband, D., and their two children, Camille and Wade.